the Three Grumpies

Alex, Ben and David – your laughter keeps my Grumpies away – *T.W.*

For Tom and Ette – *R.C.*

BLOOMSBURY
CHILDREN'S
BOOKS

First published in Great Britain in 2003 by Bloomsbury Publishing Plc
38 Soho Square, London, W1D 3HB

Text copyright © Tamra Wight 2003
Illustrations copyright © Ross Collins 2003
The moral right of the author and illustrator has been asserted

A CIP catalogue record of this book is available from the British Library
ISBN 0 7475 6423 X
Colour Separation by SC (Sang Choy) International
Printed in Hong Kong by South China Printing Co.

10 9 8 7 6 5 4 3 2 1

the Three Grumpies

by Tamra Wight illustrated by Ross Collins

BLOOMSBURY
CHILDREN'S
BOOKS

I woke up on the wrong side of the bed this morning.

"Oh my!"
said Mum.
"It looks like you
have the Grumpies
today.

Try to get
rid of them
dear."

Grumpy jiggled the table until my milk spilled. I shouted **GET OUT!**

Grumpier squeezed toothpaste everywhere.

"Dad, I have the Grumpies today!"

"Try showing them how you feel," Dad suggested.

I tried to make my lunch but Grumpy had eaten all the snacks.

I shook my fist at him.

I tried to pack
my homework,
but Grumpier
had
lost it.

I stuck my tongue out at him.

Grumpiest
tripped me
as I got
on the
bus.

SCHOOL BUS

Showing them how
I felt wasn't working.

So I put on my meanest face.

The Grumpies giggled.

All three of them.

At school Grumpy broke all my favourite crayons.

Then Grumpier squished my lunch flat.

In art Grumpiest spattered paint

on my new shirt.

The Grumpies smiled. All three of them.

Grumpy tripped me as I got off the bus.

Grumpier kept

I looked to the right and hummed.

"Mum, the Grumpies are still here!"
"Oh dear!" said Mum. She looked a little frazzled.

I smiled a little weary smile.

But the Grumpies didn't smile.
In fact they looked a little
nervous.

All three of them.

So...when Grumpy made
mud in the sandbox,

When Grumpier dumped
my green beans
on the floor,

I giggled at him.

The next thing I knew, the Grumpies were waving goodbye.

All three of them.

"What a grumpy day," I said to Mum as she kissed me goodnight.

I wonder who
will get the Grumpies next?